PERPLEXITY

KADARI LINGASWAMY

Made with ❤ on the Notion Press Platform
www.notionpress.com

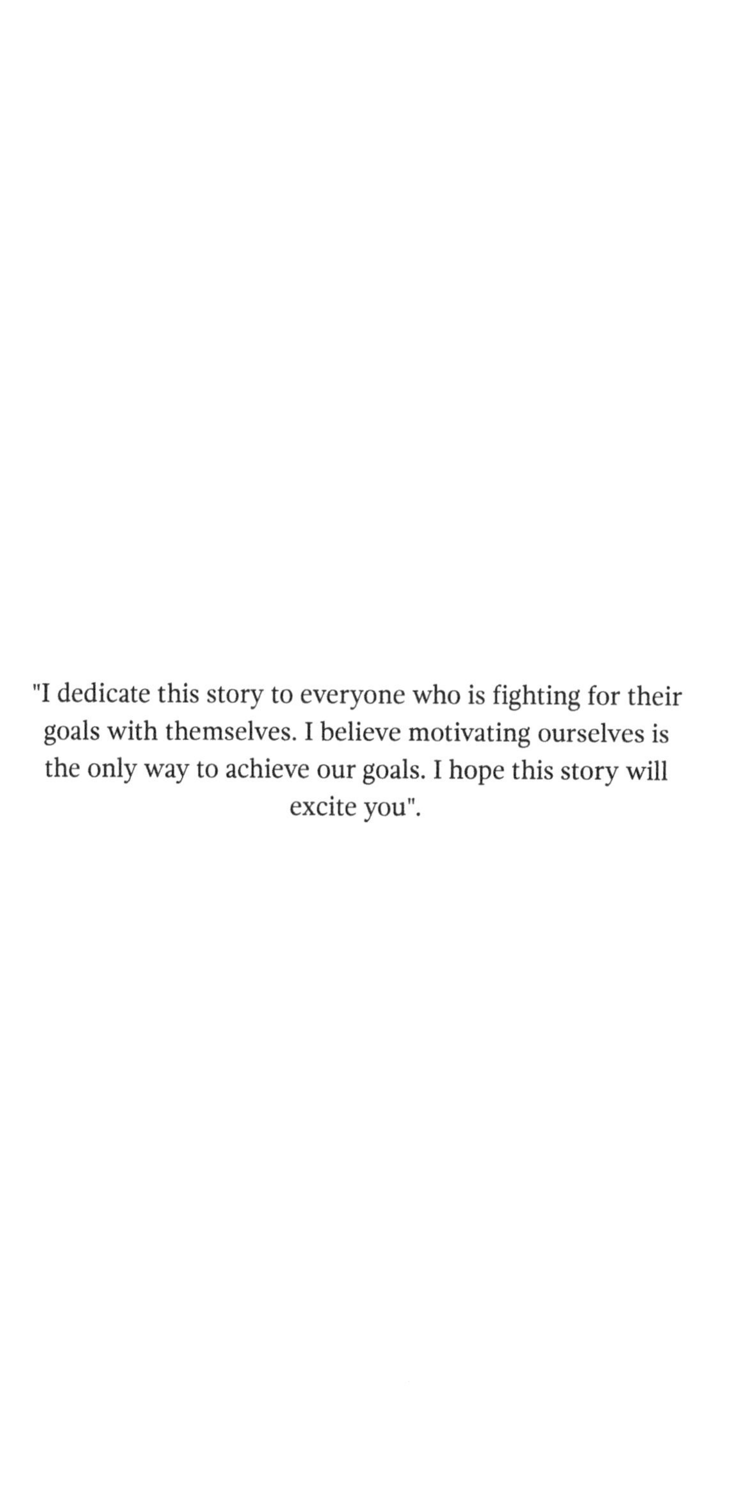

"I dedicate this story to everyone who is fighting for their goals with themselves. I believe motivating ourselves is the only way to achieve our goals. I hope this story will excite you".

Contents

Contents

Preface

I am a writer who wanted to tell stories with an intriguing screenplay and a message.

This story is about a boy named Rahul. He is getting strange dreams from summer. The strangeness in dreams was expanding and made him confused. He understood that he can know his future through his dreams. He thinks it is a power but it becomes a curse for him. He remembers nothing about his past. His problems increased with time and made his life complicated. How he finds solutions to his problems? HOW and WHEN it started?

Foreword

Dear readers,

For a long time, Lingaa, as we friends call him, and I have had discussions and endless debates on more things than many;

ranging from politics to thermodynamics. He has a keen eye for knowledge in depth. Especially history and culture of not only India but of the world. He patiently slides in his philosophical takes even on mundane topics every chance he gets in a discussion. I often admired how he could effortlessly make time for writing given his hectic schedule of a life to make his ends meet. I'm convinced now - it's his creative yearning to write. An irresistible urge to write. Perplexity is a crescent of Lingaa's imaginative and clustered mind. A metaphysical thriller that runs into a philosophical climax...built upon cultural anecdotes. Pay attention, read between the lines, connect the dots, try a wider view...it'll grip you well and keep you perplexed till the end.

There are great writer who aspire me to read stories and write stories.I

Acknowledgements

This is a fictional story and it is not based on any individual, caste, or religion.I sincerely apologize if anything in the story hurt your feelings.

I thank all the people who encouraged me to develop from a layman to a skilled writer. I am thankful to GOD for blessing me with creativity. I thank my family, and friends Kranthi, Praveena, and Manish, and special thanks to Kalyani dhi and Haritha dhi for their support and encouragement. I thank NOTION PRESS founders for helping and encouraging me to write and publish good stories.

A SPECIAL THANKS TO KAUSHIK.

THANK YOU ALL.

Prologue

This is a science fiction thriller. This story is all about a teenager who meets many challenges in less time. His problems are strange and unusual. He cannot discuss it with anyone because it is hard to believe. He still manages to find solutions to his problems. The problems faced by Rahul are also our problems but we need to find them ourselves. This story may be fictional but the moral of the story relates to our life.

THE BEGINNING

THE BEGINNING

CHAPTER ONE

INTRODUCTION

forest

Three young men are riding bicycles in the woods. The cold breeze is freezing them and unusual sounds scare them. They moved forward and at some distance, they saw the dead bodies of some creatures. They were scared by all these events and saw each other's faces with fear, and they saw one among them was missing. They are stunned and frightened. But one of them told that he might stop somewhere. He will meet us at the caves. So they started moving ahead. After a few meters, they met a Y junction, and one of them asked which way to go and turned back. He cannot see anyone around him. He was horrified and in the middle of the jungle. He was sweating, and his body became wet with sweat. He felt something in front of him, and he screamed. He turned to cycle back and started to ride the bicycle fast to move toward the road. Now the noise has reduced, and he is trying to increase the speed of the bicycle. He reached the road and stopped there. He was gasping and sweating because of fear. He looked around and saw a street light at some distance. When he tried to move towards it, he saw two dead bodies under it. He held his breath and moved toward the bodies and tried to see their faces with dismay. He was stunned after seeing their faces. They are his two friends whom he came there with. He started screeching and, unexpectedly, two dead people woke up and started to giggle. He understood that his friends tricked him. They played a very bad prank on him. He started beating them, and they were running, and another one was chasing them. Hi, friends. I am Rahul. I am the mastermind behind this prank. I am a crazy guy. I like fantasies very much. I like dreams. The other two are friends, Roshan and Swasthik. We completed our 11th standard. We are enjoying our holidays.

CHAPTER TWO

BORING SUMMER DAYS

(PLACE - my house; time-morning)

The phone rang (call from swastika). He said "Hi! Rahul." "Hello, Swastik, what's up? Why did you call me early in the morning?" I asked. He replied: "Some of our friends asked me to plan for trekking. What do you say?" he asked. “Yes, it is a good idea. I am feeling bored sitting at home,” he said. I got up from my bed and started brushing my teeth and tried to recollect the dreams of last night, but, strangely, I can’t recollect anything. I felt that maybe I didn’t dream anything last night. I played some games the whole day, but I felt today’s time went very slowly. I had my dinner. At night, before going to bed. Today, the whole day was boring. At least I am expecting something crazy in my dreams.

CHAPTER THREE

TREKKING WITH FRIENDS

Next day...

On the bicycle to woods

I wake up early in the morning because we have planned for trekking. My friends and I started to go to the forest on our bicycles. On the way to the forest, we met a junction and all were thinking about which way to go because there are no signboards at the junction. I suddenly felt something, and I said to take right from there. We reached somewhere in the jungles and felt we chose the wrong way. We came back to the junction and went in the right direction now. Some of my friends rebuke me for my decision to take the right side road.

Y junction

We reached a safe place, and it was night, so my friends were trying to set up our tents and campfire.. But I was thinking about the junction instead of helping them because I felt I had seen it somewhere, and I told them to take the right side road. But I can't remember anything. I tried to forget it for a moment and enjoy time with friends. My friends are at a campfire. They were discussing childhood stories that scared them. I went there after some time, and one of my friends asked me to tell one childhood story of mine. I said okay and tried to remember, but my mind became blank. I felt as if I was not able to remember anything. I stood silent because I did not remember anything, but they continued. We had our dinner and slept. I was not able to sleep with these doubts. But I slept somehow because of tiredness.

CHAPTER FOUR

RAHUL A SAVIOR

Next sunrise we enjoyed trekking, and some of my friends want to go to the waterfalls. In the evening we went to the waterfalls. By seeing the waterfalls, I felt that I had seen it somewhere, and it was not safe. I said to my friends, but a few did not care about me Words and waterfalls entered waterfalls. I am feeling worried about them. I unexpectedly looked up and noticed that the water flow was increasing, and I dragged my friends back. We started to gasp after the incident because it would be a miserable incident if I couldn't responded quickly. They thanked me for saving them. We left for home before dusk. I was going to bed, and I remembered that I saw waterfalls in the dream, and one of my friends was sweeping with the water flow. But I was not sure because it is not clear.

CHAPTER FIVE

My Mysterious Dreams

After a few days....

From tomorrow college will begin, and I felt I had done nothing crazy in summer vacation. I am getting strange dreams, sometimes I feel glad and worried sometimes. With time strangeness is expanding in my dreams, and I am feeling my dreams are becoming false (opposite to reality). On the first day of college, I woke up, and I was getting ready for college. I remembered that last night in my dream I forgot to take my assignment with me to college. So I make sure that it is in my bag. I wanted to tell my friends about strange dreams. But before that, I wanted to test it. I went to college, and the first day was good. I was anxious to go to bed and to dream. It was night, and I had my dinner and slept.

CHAPTER SIX

RAHUL A SUPER HERO

Next day.....

I was going to school on my bicycle, and I saw an old man on the way, and suddenly something came to my mind. I ran to him and held him for some time because last night I dreamt that this old man had died in an accident. Now I am pretty sure about the dream because I can recognize his face very well, and a truck came there, and it was out of control. I saved him from the accident. Now I am feeling proud of myself and feeling like a hero. I decided to tell about my dreams to my friends. I told my friends that I was getting strange dreams, and it was happening quite opposite of the reality. They chuckled and made fun of me and teased me by calling me a daydreamer. I felt embarrassed. I went home and said to my parents about my strange dreams, and they laughed at me. Usually, I used to make fun of everyone, but today for the first time my friends poke fun at me. I felt no one would believe me. So I decided not to tell anyone about this.

CHAPTER SEVEN

RAHUL PROPOSED RIYA

Next morning. My parents were calm. They spoke nothing about my dreams. When I went to school, and my friends were also silent, I felt relief that they forgot about my dreams. I spoke about different topics with them. We were discussing. One of my friends told me that Riya loved me, and he told me to propose to her. In the beginning, I hesitated to propose. But they motivated me to propose to her by saying she was my crush, and it is now the right time to propose to her. I finally got convinced because it is my last year in school. So I proposed to her. She smiled at me and said yes!

Rahul proposing riya

CHAPTER EIGHT

LIFE TURNS UPSIDE DOWN

A few days later. Now I am in the 12th standard. So my parents are serious about my education, and they warned me to stop dreaming and do well in the exams. I was focusing on my education. But I keep getting dreams continuously. So I tried to stop it by trying different techniques. I finally planned to do as exactly in the dreams, and maybe it will counter my dreams. But slowly I started becoming the person in my dreams. I was a crazy boy, but now I became silent and inactive. Days are passing, and I keep getting irritated with my dreams. For the last couple of days, I could remember the whole dream which I had dreamt. I lost myself in my dreams and was not able to tell which is a dream and which is a reality. Because, first, I was dreaming of a picture, then a scene, then an hour, and now the whole day.

Rahul in depression

Days are passing, and my problem is increasing. One day, I saw someone proposing to Riya, and she accepted it. I was shocked and went to her and asked about my proposal. She behaved as if she didn't know anything about my proposal. I felt strange, and I asked my friends: "If you remember that the next day after I told you about my strange dreams, I proposed to Riya. "What! You proposed to Riya, but when?"After the day I told you about my strange dreams. No, you never told us about strange dreams in recent times. I was shocked, and I started to sweat. I ran to the house and asked my parents"If I told you about my strange dreams." They replied, "No, you didn't". I was stunned, and it took me some time to digest it, and then I tried to figure it out. Finally, I got to know that all these things happened in my dreams and not in the reality. But I don't know what to do.

CHAPTER NINE

BOOKS ARE OUR DEAREST FRIENDS

Now I am more worried about myself. I am going through serious depression, but I stood strong. I wanted to find a solution to my problem myself. Because even if I went to a psychologist, it may become my dream. So first I need to find what reality is and what is the dream. The next morning I went to the central library and took some psychology books. I started reading those books. I got to the conclusion that meditation can give me some mental relief. I saw somewhere in the books that believing something strongly can make it possible if the subconscious brain believes it. I practiced and waited patiently. Then I can come outside of my dreams. I did it exactly, and with God's grace, I got out of it.

CHAPTER TEN

IT'S THE BEGINNING OF A DISASTER.

In the hospital

So, I decided to go to a psychologist and try to know about my problem. I had an appointment with a psychologist and sat in the corridor. I was waiting for my turn, and I saw a whiteboard with a quote on the wall. I paused there for a few seconds because it was interesting and confusing at the same time. Suddenly, someone said, "sir, it's your turn."I met the psychologist and explained my problem. He asked "did you have any head injuries before?" I said, "No, I didn't". He asked, "please tell me when you have this problem?" I said, "since last summer I was facing these problems". He asked me to tell him something about my childhood. I was not able to tell anything because my mind was empty, and I couldn't remember anything from before the summer holidays. He was silent for some time and then wrote some medicine. But I did not get answers to my doubts. I went out thinking about why I was not able to remember things that happened before summer. My eyes again dropped to the whiteboard. I felt that it was somehow related to me, and I kept thinking of it. It is written as "you are not a fake, and you are not real".

Mysterious quote on board.

PERPLEXITY-CONTINUOUS

PERPLEXITY-CONTINUOUS

CHAPTER ELEVEN

NIGHT MARE

I sat in the hospital and kept thinking that how can I find answers to all my questions. Suddenly, something came into my mind, and I got a question: if I could not remember my past, then who knows my past? Then I got the answer that I could know from my friends and parents. I wanted to ask my parents about this. So I went to my house. But I couldn't find my parents in the house. So I tried to ask my neighbor. I was shocked after listening to their words. Because they said, they didn't know me. I started to sweat with fear, and I went to school looking for my friends, but, strangely, I couldn't find them anywhere in the college. I felt something fishy and ran to the office room. I was shocked after checking the register because I did not find my name and my friend's names in the register.

Thinking deep

CHAPTER TWELVE

MYSTERIOUS WORLD

I sat there and started recollecting all the things that happened in my life for a few days. I thought maybe my dreams could answer my questions. So I was waiting for bedtime. It is night now, and I am eager to go to bed. Finally, I went to bed and tried to get some sleep. But I was not able to fall asleep because of my anxiety. I slowly fell into sleep with these thoughts. Next morning... I woke up, and I was brushing my teeth. I try to remember my last night's dream. But surprisingly, no dream came into my mind. I felt that I was dreaming again but this time with more reality. So I wanted to know whether I am dreaming. So I tried to verify it." I asked everyone here: "Is this a dream?"But they looked at my face for some time and started laughing. It seemed weird to me. I feel I am in a dream and want to wait for the end of my dreams. But there is no clue that this is a dream. It is only my hope. After a few days, It's already been a week, and I still don't know what was happening around me. I feel that I entered a new world with no friends and family. I wanted to know what what was happening. So, I thought of writing a book on my life and wanted to name it“you are not a fake, and you are not real".

CHAPTER THIRTEEN

MEETING A MYSTERIOUS OLD MAN

I wanted to write this book because the person who knows me will contact me, and the person who knows the meaning of the quote will respond to me. I wrote the book, and I am waiting for the response, but no one contacted me. Suddenly, one day an old man came to me and said"I know you." But I didn't know the person, and I have never seen him in any of my dreams. I asked him "how do you know me?" He said, "you met with an accident. I saw you there, and you are in a dream now". I asked him"whose dream was this?" He said: "you are dreaming yourself". I asked, "How to come outside of this dream?" He said, "you know that". I wanted to ask him how he entered my dream, but he vanished unexpectedly before I asked him.

Rahul with a mysterious old man

CHAPTER FOURTEEN

TOWARDS A HAPPY ENDING

So now it is clear that I am in a dream. I wanted to come out of this dream. So I meditated for some time to remember the technique to come out of the dream. I remembered that what you believe is you. If I believe that I am dreaming, then I will become a dream, and if my subconscious mind believes that I am not in a dream, then I will come out of my dream. So I tried to do so. I successfully came out of the dream, and I woke up.

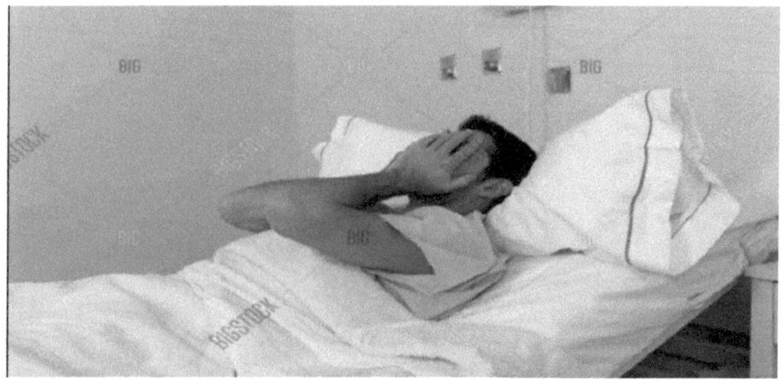

Rahul on the hospital bed

I found myself in a hospital bed. I met the doctor and asked him "how did I come here?" He said, "you met with an accident, and you were in a coma." I asked: "Is this real or am I dreaming?" He replied "this is real. You were in a coma, so you feel like you are dreaming." I tried to remember my past, but I couldn't remember things that happened. So I asked him "why am I not able to recollect my past?" He replied, "You met with an accident, so you had a head injury, and it damaged your memory." After speaking to the doctor, it was clear that I was in reality. I went to my house, and I found my parents' backs. After seeing my parents back, I felt relieved, and, lastly, I wanted to see my friends. So I was waiting for the next day.

CHAPTER FIFTEEN

BACK TO GOLDEN DAYS

Next day.....

I had good sleep last night and no dreams. I went to my school, and I met my friends there. I am feeling very happy now. For the last few days, I have been very much depressed because of incidents that took place in my life. I went back home happily. I am feeling everything has come back to normal. I feel I will get good sleep today after clearing all my problems.

CHAPTER SIXTEEN

IT IS BACK

Next day. I woke up early this morning because I got a dream again. In my dream, I saw the quote again and the person who helped me to come out of my dreams. My head is severely pained because of the dreams and stresses thinking about it. So I tried to ignore it by involving in some work. Days are passing, and I am enjoying life like a crazy person. I am preparing for my 12th exams, and very soon I am going to write my exams. But still, sometimes I get strange dreams (false dreams) and most of the time a quote on the whiteboard. So I decided to find solutions after my exams. After a few days, I completed my 12th exam and wanted to do BA psychology, but my parents wanted me to do B-tech. Meanwhile, I want to clarify my doubt about the mysterious quote and the mysterious person in my dreams.

CHAPTER SEVENTEEN

THE ASTONISHING TRUTH

I went to the hospital to see the quote again, but there is no such quote, and I got no information about it from the hospital. I searched on google and, strangely, there is no such quote. Finally, I want to find the meaning myself. So I started to crack the code behind" U are not fake, and you are not real" and what its relation is to me. I tried a lot, but I understood nothing, and I felt time could only answer my question. A few days later... I am cleaning my room and clearing all the unwanted documents and old newspapers. Suddenly, I saw my picture in an old newspaper.When I started reading the news, I was astonished because it is about my accident. After reading the newspaper, I got to know that I met with an accident after coming from the hospital.So I realized that I had to know my past. I was going to my parents to ask about it. Unexpectedly, I fell down the stairs and injured myself.

Rahul reading the news paper.

CHAPTER EIGHTEEN

CRACKING THE CODE

Next day...

I woke up with a phone call from Swastik, he was saying we passed our 12th standard exams with good results.

I got up from my bed, and I went to brush my teeth. I am brushing my teeth and recollecting my last night's dream, and I remembered the old man who helped me to come out of the dream saying one sentence this time in my dream. So I immediately took a paper and tried to recollect and note it on the paper.

It is "you are real because you feel that you are real, and you are fake because you are not real". I am already fed up with one code and a new code now. But I feel that he wants to help me and wants to tell me something.

So I wrote all my questions on a piece of paper and tried to find the link between them. When I tried to crack the second code, I found it was related to the first one.

The second code is "I am real because I feel that I am real, which means I am REAL, and I am not fake because I am not real, which means I am FAKE."The first code is "you are not fake, means REAL, and you are not real, means FAKE".

I finally cracked the second code, which is the meaning of the first code, which means I am not real. What! I am not real. I feel this is impossible because just a few days back I woke up from the dream, and now I feel normal except for some strange dreams at night.

I am thinking about why everything is happening to me, and I wanted to ask my friends about my past tomorrow.

CHAPTER NINETEEN

A SERIES OF MISFORTUNES

Next morning...

I woke up early this morning because of a strange dream, and this time I saw myself as silent and dull. Someone is calling me but with a different name. I felt weird and tried to ignore it. Because first, I wanted to know my past.

I wanted to ask my friend Roshan about my past, and I am on the way to his house. Suddenly, a few people came in front of my bicycle. They tried to kidnap me, and I ran back to my house.

I don't know why someone is trying to abduct me. I don't have any enemies.

I was thinking about the incidents that took place in the last few days. First, my accident, then I found a newspaper, then I fell down the stairs, and now someone tried to kidnap me. I kept thinking and thinking but understood nothing.

But when I compared the incidents and situations, I found something common, and it blew my mind. Because whenever I am trying to know my past, something is happening to me. First, they confused me with an accident, and the second time I fell, and now someone tries to kidnap me. Who is this? Why is he trying to stop me from knowing my past?

PERPLEXITY-THE CONCLUSION

THE CONCLUSION

CHAPTER TWENTY

ENLIGHTENMENT

Next morning.....

I am in my bed at home. I opened my eyes, and it was dark everywhere. I can't see anything, and I try to switch on the lights, but there is no switch here.

A cool breeze is blowing, and I am feeling cold. So I try to close windows and doors. But strangely, I found no doors. I understood why there were no doors or windows, and I was astonished because I was somewhere else and not in my house. I can't see anything except darkness.

Through darkness

I am more tensed and confused. But I try to keep my mind calm and try to think by closing my eyes. After some time, when I opened my eyes, I saw a light far away from me. I ran towards it and tried to reach the light. I ran for miles, but still, it is far away. I was exhausted and fell to my knees.

I cried out loudly and unexpectedly, a man came in front of me, and his face was glowing, so I couldn't see his face.

BRIGHTER SIDE

That man with a sweet voice said "you can't just run from the darkness because it is everywhere, and it is even within you. So don't try to escape from it. Rather, search for the light. First, lose your ignorance, then you can automatically see the brightness because ignorance is darkness.

"Please stop this nonsense, I am fed up with this. Tell me who you are. Why are you saying all these things to me? Do you know who is stopping me from getting to know my past?"I asked.

"Please be calm. Keep your mind pleasant because it is your only friend of yours," he replied.

"First, answer me: where am I? Who is stopping me from knowing the truth?"I asked.

"I will not answer your questions because you have all the answers," he replied.

"I don't know, please tell me?"I asked.

"Your mind is the doorway for all the questions and your thoughts were the keys to it," he replied.

"I don't know anything, please tell me. I begged."

I kept asking the same question in a loud voice and started to shout at him.

He vanished from here with a smile, and I tried to hold him tightly. Suddenly, I felt like I felt from somewhere, and I saw myself on the floor, beside the bed. I rubbed my eyes, and it is morning. I understood that everything was a dream.

CHAPTER TWENTY-ONE

A DISTURBING SMILE

I woke up from bed and started brushing my teeth. I am feeling a severe headache after the dream, so I had a cup of coffee and trying to do some work to keep myself busy and ignore my dream. But the smile in my dream is disturbing me every time.

The whole day went by ignoring the dream, and I am not able to sleep and became restless.

I tried to keep my mind calm, and then a sentence came into my mind: "you can't run from darkness because it is everywhere and it is even within you, rather search for light".

Then I understood that he was telling me about myself. He wants to say do not ignore your questions rather find the solutions for them.

After understanding his sentence, I tried to recollect everything that he said in the dream.

I remembered that he said the mind was the doorway for all the answers and thoughts were the keys to opening it. I tried to concentrate on my sense and started to meditate. I heard a sound. So I try to be calm to listen to it.

Someone suddenly started to laugh and warned me. He said don't try to become smart, just forget everything and lead your life.

I am feeling that I am losing control of my mind. I asked him "who are you?". Why are you doing these things and stopping me from knowing the truth? I have to know about my past."

He smiles and says "if you try to know your past, I will kill your parents and friends. I know you don't want it. So do what I said."

I opened my eyes and thought that he was a coward, and he had no courage to come in front of me. I didn't care about his words. So I decided to meet my father and ask him about my past.

I was going to see my father get to know about my past, and suddenly I got a phone call from my mother saying that she was in the hospital, and my father met with an accident. I was terrified after listening to her and ran to the hospital to see him.

CHAPTER TWENTY-TWO

IMMORTAL

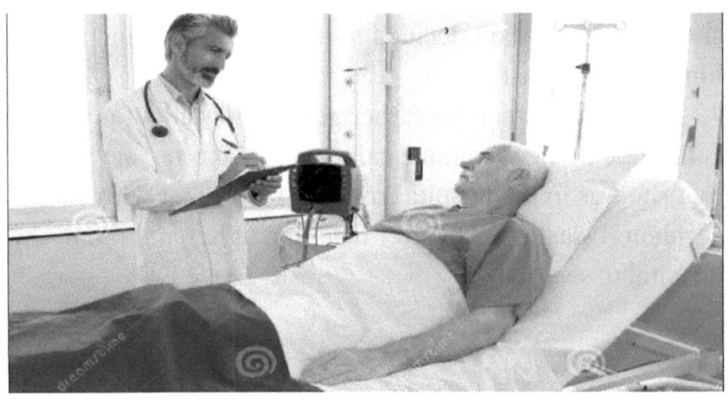

Rahul's father in hospital

I went to the hospital and saw him. When I spoke to the doctor, he said he was out of danger.I sat on a chair in the hospital with depression, and I am feeling a severe headache. I tried to close my eyes. I heard the sound of laughing again, and I tried to focus on the sound. I can hear the same sound which warned me. He said I had got the result for what you have tried to know. But this is just the beginning, so don't be foolish.

I am frightened this time because my father is in a hospital bed. So I decided to listen to his words.

I tried to ignore my questions and lead my life. My strange dreams were continuous with time. I am irritated with my life and don't want to live anymore. So I decided to commit suicide by hanging myself.

I have made everything ready. I hung myself to the rope. Slowly I am feeling suffocation, and I lost my life.

I am dead now, but I am feeling something. I realized how my brain is working. I tried to open my eyes. I was amazed because I found myself on the bed again. It has become a dream. But how is it possible? I remember everything that I had done. I am thinking about how it is possible. I understood that he was stopping me from death.

My head again started to ache, and I closed my eyes. He again started to chuckle. I can hear his laugh. I am very much irritated. By the person. I questioned him, what do you want from me? Why are you torturing me?

I am not torturing you. I want you to forget everything and lead a happy life.

I said it was impossible to live happily without finding answers to my questions.

I heard no voice again after I spoke strongly with him. I opened my eyes and decided to end this game by hook or crook.

CHAPTER TWENTY-THREE

MEETING MY PARAMATMA

Next day...

I came to the central library because I feel every question has an answer, and we can find every answer here. I took a few books which are related to psychology, the brain, and supernatural forces. I started reading and did not stop until I finished all the books.

After reading all these books, I concluded that there was no solution to my problems in these books. But I found a method to find answers to my questions. I don't have faith in any religion. But, I got to know that, according to Hinduism, by practicing deep meditation we can know the answer to the most difficult questions. I started with no confidence, but there is no other way.

So I sat on a comfortable seat and in the correct position by closing my eyes. I was trying to focus, but some other thoughts kept disturbing me. But my commitment to finding the solution crossed all the hurdles. After a few minutes, I felt lighter and the darkness in my eyes turned to bright light. All the brightness is concentrated on a point.

PARAMATMA

I heard a melodious voice calling me from the bright spot. I went near it and asked him "who are you?

"I am you, and you are me," he replied.

"I think you are Paramatma, whom I want to meet," I said.

"Yes! I am," he said.

"I want to get to know the person who is torturing me, "I asked.

"That is you whom you are searching for" he answered."

"What!"(expressed).

"Yes! The one who is torturing you is yourself and you, you feel is not real," he replied.

"You are in a lucid dream, which means the real you are dreaming, and you are his 89th lucid dream."

It was unbelievable but after all the unbelievable things that happened in my life. I understood it very fast.

"How I can come outside of this lucid dream?"I asked. "It is only possible with the real you. When he feels happy

And he has the desire to live, and he will wake up from the dream.

And you have to sacrifice yourself for him. When he becomes real, you will turn into a fake."He explained.

"How can I make him happy?" I inquired.

"You can be happy when you accept the truth of your life," he said.

"What is the truth? I asked"

"Truth is the reality and the life of the real you," he replied. Who is the person who tried to help me?

He is also you. Every human has two sides of the brain. The one who accepts the bitter truth and the other expects a sweet lie.

Why can't I see you?

You can see me only when you had focus, a pleasant mind, and a pure soul. Everything turned dark again.

I opened my eyes, and I was in the library. I felt as if I was in dreamland for a few minutes.

After some time ,I am thinking about the real me. Why does he want to live in dreams? It is very difficult for me to decide to end this dream because it can turn my life into a lie. But I decided to sacrifice my life and wanted the real me to accept reality. I cannot live a normal life after knowing all these things. I tried to communicate with him.

CHAPTER TWENTY-FOUR

DISCOVERING MYSELF

I closed my eyes and focused on my senses. I heard the sound of the real me. I tried to talk to him.

I don't know your name, but you have given me life and relationships. I am thankful to you for all that. But now I have learned all the truth about myself. I cannot live this fake life anymore happily, and without my happiness, you cannot be happy. I want to know about you and your idea of a lucid dream. (There was silence for some time, but a voice broke the silence)

I am Ranganath. I was born into a poor family. I was a silent and innocent boy. My friends always tease me and irritate me. I have never been happy in my life. So I decided to die, but a man stopped me and told me about the lucid dream. I did not believe in his words earlier, but later I experienced it. But the lucid dream can only be possible for a limited period. I practiced it several times so that I could pause myself in a lucid dream with the desired life. You are the 89th dream, and I have the least control over you. So the other side of me tried you to realize the reality in your dreams (strange dreams). But I don't want you to come outside of the dream. He explained.

I cannot live this life anymore because I am not true. I cannot live happily anymore, and I am ready to sacrifice my life for you. I want you to accept the bitter truth (Ranganath) and forget the sweet lie (Rahul).

I tried to convince him, and he was silent because of his helplessness. Later he got convinced because there was no other way. I asked him "is it possible to end this dream?"

He asked me to close my eyes with patience and wait until I heard a beep sound. I said OK.

I closed my eyes, and I started to recollect all the things and happy moments which happened in my life. I am feeling emotional. I am sacrificing my friends, family, and you all. Maybe these are my last words to you all. “YOU dream of something which changes your life but with open eyes and works hard to achieve it”.

"Bye, everyone, I love you all".

I closed my eyes tightly so that I do not feel the desire to live again in dreams.

Ranganath opened his eyes and found himself in his house.

For his dreams but not for his thoughts

What Dharma Says

According to Sanathana Dharma...

"In Satya-Yuga, the enemy was in the other world.

In Thretha-Yuga, the enemy was on another continent.

In Dwapara-Yuga, the enemy was in the family.

And now in Kali-Yuga, the enemy is within you."

So don't encourage the negativity within you to grow. It is only possible with the right thoughts, right beliefs, and right actions.

Thank you for reading...

--K.Lingaswamy

Printed by Libri Plureos GmbH in Hamburg, Germany